AND THE
QUEST FOR THE
MAGIC PORCUPINE

**Look for Stinkbomb and
Ketchup-Face's other kerfuffles:**

❧ · ❧

Stinkbomb and Ketchup-Face
and the Badness of Badgers

Stinkbomb and Ketchup-Face
and the Pizza of Peril

JOHN DOUGHERTY

STINKBOMB
and
Ketchup-Face
AND THE
QUEST FOR THE
MAGIC PORCUPINE

ILLUSTRATED BY SAM RICKS

PUFFIN BOOKS

PUFFIN BOOKS

An imprint of Penguin Random House LLC
375 Hudson Street
New York, New York 10014

First published in Great Britain by Oxford University Press in 2014
First published in the United States of America by G. P. Putnam's Sons,
an imprint of Penguin Random House LLC, 2018
Published by Puffin Books, an imprint of Penguin Random House LLC, 2019

THE LIBRARY OF CONGRESS HAS CATALOGED THE G. P. PUTNAM'S SONS EDITION AS FOLLOWS:
Names: Dougherty, John, author. | Ricks, Sam, illustrator.
Title: Stinkbomb and Ketchup-Face and the quest for the magic porcupine / John
Dougherty ; illustrated by Sam Ricks.
Description: First American edition. | New York, NY : G. P. Putnam's Sons, 2018. |
"First published in Great Britain by Oxford University Press."
Summary: "Stinkbomb and his sister, Ketchup-Face, fulfill a quest to find the
Magic Porcupine in hopes of capturing the escaped rascally badgers"—Provided
by publisher.
Identifiers: LCCN 2016044470 | ISBN 9781101996652 (hardcover)
Subjects: | CYAC: Brothers and sisters—Fiction. | Adventure and adventurers—
Fiction. | Badgers—Fiction. | Magic—Fiction. | Humorous stories.
Classification: LCC PZ7.D74433 Stq 2018 | DDC [Fic]—dc23
LC record available at https://lccn.loc.gov/2016044470

Puffin Books ISBN 9781101996669

Printed in the United States of America.

Design by Eileen Savage.
Text set in Warnock Pro.

As always, to Noah and Cara, without whom there would be no Stinkbomb & Ketchup-Face. (There would still be badgers. But probably not these particular badgers.)—J. D.

For Mom and Dad. —S. R.

What happened in *Stinkbomb and Ketchup-Face and the Badness of Badgers*
by STINKBOMB

My sister Ketchup-Face and I went on an adventure, armed only with our wits and a few really useful things I happened to have in my pockets.

We were brave and clever and we found the villainous badgers—who dig holes in the lawn and eat all the worms, and knock over garbage cans, and frighten chickens and drive too fast—and stopped them from doing their evil and wicked doings. In the end we got them thrown in jail, and we did it all by ourselves.

Well, nearly all by ourselves. A few people helped us.

There was King Toothbrush Weasel, who's the king of Great Kerfuffle, the island where we live. And a little shopping cart who isn't a horse, whatever my sister says. And the army of Great Kerfuffle, too, but that's not as impressive as it sounds because he's just a small cat named Malcolm the Cat.

Anyway, it was a great book. You should read it.

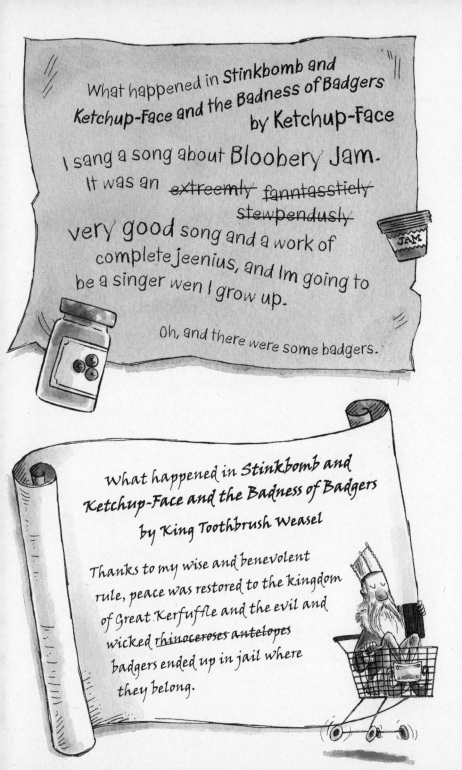

What happened in *Stinkbomb and Ketchup-Face and the Badness of Badgers* by Ketchup-Face

I sang a song about Bloobery Jam. It was an ~~extreemly~~ ~~fanntasstiely~~ ~~stewpendusly~~ very good song and a work of complete jeenius, and Im going to be a singer wen I grow up.

Oh, and there were some badgers.

What happened in *Stinkbomb and Ketchup-Face and the Badness of Badgers* by King Toothbrush Weasel

Thanks to my wise and benevolent rule, peace was restored to the kingdom of Great Kerfuffle and the evil and wicked ~~rhinoceroses~~ ~~antelopes~~ badgers ended up in jail where they belong.

What happened in

Stinkbomb and Ketchup-Face and the Badness of Badgers

by Malcolm the Cat

Actually, I'm not going to tell you.

Or perhaps I will.

No, maybe not.

On the other hand . . .

But then again . . .

CHAPTER I

· — ·

IN WHICH
OUR STORY BEGINS

It was a dark and stormy night on the island of Great Kerfuffle, and in the village of Loose Pebbles the streets were deserted. Nothing could be heard but the **lashing** of the rain, and the **crashing** of the thunder, and the **thrashing** of the wind.

The rain **lashed**, and the thunder **crashed**, and the wind **thrashed**; and then they **lashed** and **crashed** and **thrashed** some more.

After a bit the rain tried **thrashing**, and the thunder tried **lashing**, and the wind had a go at **crashing**, but it sounded stupid. So they swapped back, and the rain went on **lashing**, and the thunder went on **crashing**, and the wind went on **thrashing**.

And that was about it, really. After about half an hour, it became clear that the whole story had started too early. So it waited for a bit, and then started again.

CHAPTER I

·

IN WHICH
OUR STORY BEGINS AGAIN,
AND THE VILLAINOUS BADGERS
ESCAPE FROM PRISON

It was a dark and stormy night on the island of Great Kerfuffle, and in the village of Loose Pebbles the streets were deserted. Nothing could be heard but the **lashing** of the rain, and the **crashing** of the thunder, and the **thrashing** of the wind—until the story started and, in the village jail, something stirred.

The village jail was full of badgers. They had been there since the end of the last story, and they were bored, because there was nothing to do but drive the little car **too fast** around the Monopoly board, knocking over all the houses and hotels. They had once tried playing the game properly, but it was no fun because the smallest of them, Stewart the Badger, had eaten all the pretend money.

Now most of the badgers were staring gloomily through the prison bars at the **pouring** rain. A few were driving the little dog *too fast* around the board just for variety's sake, but they weren't really enjoying it, and two were sitting in a corner with the little top hat, trying to imagine it was a garbage can and taking turns knocking it over. Stewart the Badger was **snuffling** through the Monopoly box looking for something else to eat, but he found nothing

except a lot of pink- and peach-colored cards. He nibbled thoughtfully on the corner of one, pretending it was a worm, but it just didn't have the same wriggly quality that made worms so tasty. He tried another corner in case it was any different, but it wasn't.

Just as he was about to try a third corner, the card was snatched from his paw.

"What's this?" Harry the Badger asked gruffly.

"It's not a worm," Stewart the Badger explained. "Or a garbage can."

"I can see that," said Harry the Badger, turning it over and grinning a badgerish grin. "It's even better than worms and garbage cans!"

"**Ooooh,**" said all the other badgers, suddenly interested. They didn't know anything *could* be better than worms and garbage cans. "What is it?"

"You'll see," said Harry the Badger, strolling over to the door in a way that he hoped made him look cool. "Now all we need is a handy passerby."

As it happened, somebody was just about to

pass by the jail. His name was Blimey O'Reilly. He was out on this miserable night because he was going to visit his best friend, Gordon Bennett, and he was struggling onward under the **lashing** of the rain, and the **crashing** of the thunder, and the **thrashing** of the wind, and the **flashing** of the **lightning**, and the **bashing** of the bats. The bats were **bashing** into him quite a lot, because their ears had gotten all filled up with rain and they couldn't hear where they were going.

"Hey!" said Harry the Badger. "Let us out!"

"Please," added Rolf the Badger, a big badger with a big badge that said

He didn't think being polite would make any difference, but he was anxious to make his first appearance in the story before the end of the chapter.

"Ooh, no," said Blimey O'Reilly. "The king said

you had to stay in prison until the end of the next book."

"I know," said Harry the Badger. "But that was before we found . . . this!"

He held up the card he had taken from Stewart the Badger. It said:

Blimey O'Reilly read it carefully. "Does it still count if the corners have been nibbled?" he asked.

"Oh, yes," said Harry the Badger persuasively, and all the other badgers nodded and tried to look sincere.

"Oh," said Blimey O'Reilly. "All right, then." And he opened the jail door.

"Ha!" said Harry the Badger. "Free at last!"

"Yay!" cried all the other badgers, and they rushed out of the cold gray prison into the world, free badgers once more.

Then they rushed back in again. **"Yuk!"** they said. "It's raining!"

Harry the Badger rolled his eyes. "What does a bit of rain matter," he said, "compared to freedom?"

"But it's *cold*," the other badgers complained. Harry the Badger sighed and turned to Blimey O'Reilly. "Can we borrow your umbrella?" he asked.

"Please?" added Rolf the Badger, for much the same reason as before.

"Um, okay," said Blimey O'Reilly, handing it over. "But it's not very big. You won't all fit underneath it."

"Oh, yes, we will," said the badgers, as they scurried outside again and formed themselves into a **tall thin** badger tower with Harry the Badger at the top holding the umbrella.

Then Blimey O'Reilly struggled wetly onward, to a house around the corner where Gordon Bennett and his girlfriend, Maya Goodness, were waiting for him. And the tottering stack of badgers, claws glistening in the rain, wobbled off to the woods to plan some **evil** and **wicked** doings to do **evilly** and **wickedly**.

CHAPTER 2

— · —

IN WHICH
STINKBOMB AND KETCHUP-FACE WAKE UP

The sun had risen high, and the clouds had blown away. Birds were **chirruping** in the treetops, lambs were **frolicking** in the fields, squirrels were happily throwing nuts at one another, and a class of excited little maggots was having a party in a dead rat in a corner of the backyard.

The backyard belonged to a lovely house on a hillside overlooking the little village of Loose Pebbles, and inside the lovely house, in a beautiful pink bedroom, a little girl called Ketchup-Face was **snoring** like a steamroller.

In the tree outside Ketchup-Face's bedroom, a blackbird was singing. Normally, this would have been enough to wake Ketchup-Face, but on this particular morning it wasn't. So the blackbird flew away, and came back with a trumpet.

Perching on the branch nearest the window, it raised the trumpet to its beak and blew an exploratory **toot**. It peered into the wide bell.

It carefully polished the mouthpiece with one black-feathered wing. Then, like a world-famous soloist, it lifted the trumpet with a flourish, and **hurled** it as hard as it could at Ketchup-Face's head.

The trumpet bounced off Ketchup-Face's forehead with a

CLANG!!!

Ketchup-Face leapt crossly out of bed and rushed to the window.

"Hey! Blackbird!" she yelled.

The blackbird blew a **raspberry**, and flew away.

Ketchup-Face shrugged, picked up the trumpet, and crossed the landing to bother her brother. But as she entered his room, she saw something that filled her with horror.

"Stinkbomb!" she cried. "Stinkbomb! Wake up!" Stinkbomb rolled over, grunted, and said something that sounded like, "Hmmmph. Wombats."

"Wake up *now*, Stinkbomb!" Ketchup-Face pleaded, jumping onto his bed and hitting him repeatedly on the head with the trumpet.

Stinkbomb opened one bleary eye.

"What is it?" he grumbled.

"We've overslept!" Ketchup-Face wailed.

"What???" Stinkbomb exclaimed, sitting up. "What time is it?"

"It's almost Chapter Three! Look!"

Ketchup-Face yelled, pointing at the clock.

And just as she spoke, the clock began to strike.

CHAPTER 3

— · —

IN WHICH THE NEXT BIT OF STORY HAPPENS

The clock was still bonging **Chapter Three** as Stinkbomb and Ketchup-Face shoved themselves into their clothing.

"Okay!" Stinkbomb said. "We have to get on with the story."

"Yes," Ketchup-Face agreed. "What are we supposed to be doing?"

Just at that moment, there was a knock on the door.

"Hurray!" said Ketchup-Face, rushing to answer it. "It must be the story! Hello!" she added, flinging the door open. "It's King Toothbrush Weasel!"

"I am not King Toothbrush Weasel," said King Toothbrush Weasel. "I am the royal trumpeter." He pointed at his badge, which said Royal Trumpeter, and then he went:

"Toot toot toot tooty-toooot, toot toot toot toooooooooooooooot!"

Stinkbomb looked at him with interest. "Shouldn't you have a trumpet?" he said.

King Toothbrush Weasel gave him a hard stare. "I *do* have a trumpet," he said. "It's probably the best trumpet in the world. It's too good to take outdoors, that's for sure."

"Well, you ought to have a second-best one, then," Ketchup-Face said. "Have this." And she gave him the one the blackbird had thrown at her.

"Oh, thank you," said King Toothbrush Weasel. He put it to his ear and went:

"Toot toot toot tooty-toooot, toot toot toot toooooooooooooooot!"

again. Then he said, "Announcing His Royal Majesty King Toothbrush Weasel, monarch of the island of Great Kerfuffle, ruler of even the little crinkly bits around the edge, and commander in chief of Malcolm the Cat.

Toot toot toot tooty-toooot, toooooooooooooooot!"

Then he took off the badge that said Royal Trumpeter and put on a badge that said King .

"Good morning, Stinkbomb and Ketchup-Face," he said gravely. "Bad news! The badgers have escaped from prison!"

"Oh," said Stinkbomb disappointedly. "Is this *another* story about the badgers? I wanted to be in a story about zombies this time."

"What are zombies?" Ketchup-Face asked.

"They're sort of like crocodiles, but with two humps instead of one," King Toothbrush Weasel said.

"Um . . . that's camels," Stinkbomb told him.

"Nonsense!" said King Toothbrush Weasel. "Camels are nothing like zombies. Zombies can't fly. And they don't hang upside-down in dark caves."

"But that's bats," Stinkbomb said.

"Bats," said King Toothbrush Weasel firmly, "are what you hit golf balls with when you're playing tennis. But that's not important. What's important is that we've got to catch the badgers and put them back in prison before they do any evil and wicked doings."

"How?" Ketchup-Face asked.

King Toothbrush Weasel's face fell. "I thought *you'd* know," he said. He took off his crown and scratched his head. Then he scratched Stinkbomb's and Ketchup-Face's heads, and then he tugged thoughtfully at his long golden beard until it came off in his hand. "Wait a minute!" he yelped suddenly. "I've got it!"

"No, you've dropped it," said Ketchup-Face, picking up the beard and helping him put it back on.

"No, not the beard," said King Toothbrush Weasel. "I mean I've got an idea. We *are* in a story, aren't we?"

"Yes," said Stinkbomb. "Most of the way through **Chapter Three**."

"Right," said King Toothbrush Weasel. "So to find the badgers, we need someone who knows about stories!"

"Of course!" said Stinkbomb and Ketchup-Face together.

"Yes!" said King Toothbrush Weasel dramatically. "So, we need to go to . . . the post office!"

"Oh," said Stinkbomb. "I thought you were going to say *the library*."

CHAPTER 4

IN WHICH
OUR HEROES DON'T GO
TO THE POST OFFICE

J ust then, it began to rain.

It was not an ordinary rain. It was a horrible, inky-splattery, thick wet rain that left dark splotches on the ground and **smelled** faintly of bananas.

"What's happening?" said King Toothbrush Weasel.

"I bet it's got something to do with those badgers!" said Ketchup-Face.

"Why?" asked Stinkbomb, putting up an umbrella he had just found in his pocket.

"Because," explained Ketchup-Face patiently, "they're the bad guys."

"That settles it!" said King Toothbrush Weasel. "To the royal carriage—quickly!"

Outside the gate, waiting patiently, was a little shopping cart with a sticker saying **ROYAL CARRIAGE** stuck to its handle, and a small gray cat wearing a red soldier's jacket and a bored expression.

"Starlight!" said Ketchup-Face delightedly, for this was none other than the little shopping cart who wasn't actually called Starlight at all, who had helped them in their last adventure.

"And Malcolm the Cat!" she added, for the cat was none other than Malcolm the Cat, who was a small cat named Malcolm the Cat, but who was also the entire army of the little kingdom of Great Kerfuffle.

"Hello," said the little shopping cart shyly as they got in. "Where to, Your Majesty?"

"To the post office!"

commanded King Toothbrush Weasel.

"Certainly," said the little shopping cart. "Um ... why are we going to the post office?"

"Because," said King Toothbrush Weasel impatiently, "we need someone who knows about stories, and that means a butcher, and where would we find a butcher but in a post office?"

"Ah," said the little

shopping cart wisely, setting off at a **squeaky-wheeled gallop**, and before this sentence had finished they were pulling up outside the **Loose Pebbles Library**.

"Here we are," said King Toothbrush Weasel. "The post office! Filled from end to end with all manner of books, and run by the person who knows more about stories than anyone else—the butcher!"

"But it's the—**OW!**" said Ketchup-Face, as Stinkbomb jabbed her sharply in the ribs. "What did you do that for? I was only going to say that it's the—**OW!** Stop it! Why don't you want me to say that it's the—**OW!**"

"Shhh!" explained Stinkbomb.

"It's not the **OW**," King Toothbrush Weasel said sternly. "It's the post office. And this is where we'll find out how to stop the badgers doing their **evil** and **wicked** doings."

"But it's the—**OW!**" yelped Ketchup-Face crossly.

"It doesn't matter what we call it," Stinkbomb hissed, rubbing his elbow. "Let's just go in and find the librarian."

"All right," muttered Ketchup-Face. "But it *is* the—**OW!**"

The Loose Pebbles Library was the grandest building in Great Kerfuffle—much grander than the Royal Palace, which was really just a small cottage with a couple of thatched turrets stuck on and a cat in a soldier's jacket standing guard outside. This was because the only sensible king that Great Kerfuffle had ever had—who was called King Sensible—had realized that libraries are much more important than palaces.

So King Sensible had ordered every spare penny in the kingdom to be spent on building a wonderful library. And a hundred years later, the only sensible queen that Great Kerfuffle had ever had—who was called Queen Fairly Daft, because her parents considered Queen Sensible a silly name—had ordered it to be filled with books. This came as a great relief to the librarians, who had been sitting around for a hundred years waiting for something to do.

Now Stinkbomb and Ketchup-Face and King Toothbrush Weasel and Malcolm the Cat were gazing up at this majestic building, hearts filled with awe, as the sinister banana-scented rain **splottered** and **spattered** around them.

CHAPTER 5

——— • ———

IN WHICH
OUR HEROES ENTER THE LIBRARY
AND MEET MISS BUTTERWORTH

Their feet went **click, click, click** on the marbled flooring as they entered the library.

At least King Toothbrush Weasel's did. Ketchup-Face's went **tic, tic, tic** because she was lighter and wasn't wearing impressive and kingly shoes, and Stinkbomb's went **boing, boing, boing** because he was wearing his favorite boots with the bouncy soles, and Malcolm the Cat's went   ,   ,   because he was a cat.

Inside, the library was like a vast and silent cathedral of knowledge, except for the children's

section, which was full of toddlers and their parents who had come for

Bouncy Sing & Clap Story Time
with Miss Tibbles,

and which was more like a brightly colored and
noisy cathedral of dribbly fun.

"I wonder where the librarian is?" whispered
Stinkbomb.

"*I am here,*" murmured a voice like the tin-
kling of wind chimes, and suddenly, magically,
the librarian appeared among them.

"**OW!**" said Malcolm the Cat.

"*Oh, sorry,*" said the librarian, looking down
and taking her foot off Malcolm the Cat's tail.

The librarian was **tall** and **thin**, and dressed in
black clothing of fine silk. From a sash around her
waist hung a long sword. A black hood and scarf
covered her head so that nothing could be seen of
her face except for a pair of very sensible glasses,

behind which **twinkled**
wise, kind eyes.

She put her hands together and bowed her head in greeting. "I," she said, "am Miss Butterworth of the Ancient Order of Ninja Librarians. Greetings to you, Stinkbomb, Ketchup-Face, King Toothbrush Weasel, and Malcolm the Cat."

Stinkbomb was most impressed. "How do you know who we are?" he asked.

Miss Butterworth bowed again. "I am a librarian," she said. "We are keepers of all knowledge. We are guardians of all books and stories. Plus, we read a lot in our lunch hour. I enjoyed your first book very much. How may I help you?"

"We want to know how to find the badgers,"

Stinkbomb told her.

"They're making it rain a **big blobby splatty rain**," Ketchup-Face explained.

"Which **smells** faintly of bananas," Stinkbomb added.

"Yes!" said Ketchup-Face. "If we don't catch them soon, all of Great Kerfuffle will **SMELL** faintly of bananas, and it'll get invaded by monkeys and gorillas and elephants and hammerhead sharks."

"Hammerhead sharks don't like bananas," Stinkbomb pointed out.

"They would if they tried them," Ketchup-Face said. "If their mommies said, 'Eat up all your bananas or you won't get any sailors,' then they'd try them, and then they'd like them, and then they'd invade Great Kerfuffle."

"They don't eat sailors, either," said Stinkbomb, who was very interested in interesting things like facts. "They're bottom feeders."

"Ewww," said Ketchup-Face, who didn't know what a bottom feeder was, but could think of one or two horrid things it might be. "So would their mommies say, 'Eat up all your bananas or you won't get any bottoms'?"

"No," Stinkbomb explained. "It means they eat whatever they find lying on the bottom of the sea."

"Oh," said Ketchup-Face. "So if a sailor and a banana fell out of a boat, which would they eat first?"

"I don't know what hammerhead sharks have to do with anything!" interrupted King Toothbrush Weasel. "Nasty little creatures with too many legs. The point is, what are we going to do about the badgers?"

"Well," said Miss Butterworth slowly, *"there is one book which might help. To fetch it will be dangerous—but perhaps it is our only hope. And somebody did knock over the library garbage can last night, and it took me ages to clear up the mess."*

She took a deep breath, as if summoning her courage in preparation for some great ordeal—and then she wasn't there.

"Where did she go?" asked King Toothbrush Weasel.

"There she is!" cried Stinkbomb. Far above them, Miss Butterworth was scaling the **tall** bookcases toward a high shelf marked **451: FORBIDDEN BOOKS**.

Nimbly she climbed, dodging the traps that some ancient and long-forgotten librarian had left: a great stone ball on a chain that smashed into the bookshelf just where she had been a moment before; poisoned darts that buried themselves in the wall with a cascade of angry **phuts**; boiling lava that erupted in deadly fountains from a copy of *Top Traps to Keep Your Forbidden Books Safe*; and tribes of angry mice that appeared from behind a large encyclopedia and poked her with tiny pitchforks.

Then she was at the top of the highest bookcase, pulling a book from the very end of the topmost shelf. As she did so, the whole bookcase shook violently. Stinkbomb and Ketchup-Face gasped as Miss Butterworth was thrown backward into empty space, fifty feet or more above the ground.

CHAPTER 6

— • —

IN WHICH
MISS BUTTERWORTH IS PERFECTLY ALL RIGHT, AND THERE IS NOTHING TO WORRY ABOUT— EXCEPT FOR THE BADGERS, OF COURSE

Oh, dear!" said King Toothbrush Weasel, but even as he spoke, the Ninja Librarian skillfully turned her fall into a somersault. Like a gymnast, she twisted through the air to rebound off a large copy of *The Boingiest Trampoline in the World*. Down she came, leaping gracefully from shelf to shelf, until she alighted on the ground next to them with barely a sound.

"**OW,**" said Malcolm the Cat.

"*Oh, sorry,*" said Miss Butterworth, looking down and taking her foot off Malcolm the Cat's tail. Then she held up the book she was clutching. It was called STINKBOMB AND KETCHUP-FACE AND THE QUEST FOR THE MAGIC PORCUPINE.

Stinkbomb gasped. "Is that the story we're in now?" he asked, reaching for it.

Miss Butterworth held it out of his reach. "*You must not!*" she said seriously. "*No one without the training of a Ninja Librarian should try to read a story while they are in it. Otherwise great calamity will befall, endangering the very fabric of time and space!"*

Stinkbomb thought about this. The idea of great calamity befalling and endangering the very fabric of time and space certainly sounded interesting, but he wasn't sure he would actually like it. So he stuck his hand back in his pocket.

Ketchup-Face, meanwhile, was staring up at Miss Butterworth in **awe**. She thought that the fetching of that book was the most magnificent thing she had ever seen, and she was suddenly filled with hero worship. "I've written a song about libraries," she announced. "Would you like to hear it?"

"Yes, please," said Miss Butterworth.

"Oh," said Ketchup-Face, suddenly realizing that she hadn't written a song about libraries after all. However, she wasn't going to tell Miss Butterworth that, because it would be embarrassing. Instead, she took a deep breath, opened her mouth, and waited to see what came out.

What came out was:

"I like libraries
More than climbing trees
More than bits of cheese

More than the nice lady
in the sweet shop
who's got hairy knees

And if you ask me please
whether I'd like to go and
sit in the freeze . . . er

I'll say:

No, 'cause I want to go to the
library instead because it's not as cold as
the freezer and it's got lots of interesting
books and stuff like that and you can use the
internet and all the librarians are really nice
especially Miss Butterworth and it's all
amazing and anyone can borrow
the books and take them
home and read them . . .

Except the
Badgers!!!

That's a song about libraries," she added.

"*Well done,*" said Miss Butterworth politely, and Stinkbomb gave her a brotherly pat on the back.

"*Now,*" Miss Butterworth continued, "*stand back. Be still and quiet. What I am about to do is extremely dangerous.*" Very carefully, she opened the book. Immediately, a strange **humming** filled the air.

"*Excuse me,*" said Miss Butterworth sternly, looking at King Toothbrush Weasel.

King Toothbrush Weasel blushed, and stopped **humming**. "Sorry," he said.

Miss Butterworth returned her attention to the book.

"Does it tell us how to catch the badgers?" Stinkbomb asked.

Miss Butterworth nodded. "*But I cannot tell you yet.*"

"Why not?" Ketchup-Face asked.

"*Because first you must say, 'Why not?'*"

"I just did," Ketchup-Face pointed out.

"Yes," Miss Butterworth agreed, *"but until you say it again, I cannot tell you how to catch the badgers."*

"Why not?" Ketchup-Face asked.

"Because it is written," Miss Butterworth said, *"and all must happen as it is written."*

"But now she *has* said it again," Stinkbomb said. "So can you tell us how to catch the badgers?"

"Not yet," said Miss Butterworth. *"More must first come to pass."*

"Oh," said Stinkbomb. "Well . . . what else has got to happen?"

Miss Butterworth returned her eyes to the book and flicked silently through its pages. *"Many things will happen before the secret is revealed,"* she said. *"King Toothbrush Weasel will say, 'Eh? What?'; a mysterious stranger in a raincoat will enter the library; the Number 94 bus will go past outside; the chapter will end, and a new one must begin; Malcolm the Cat will say 'ow'; and then, on page 46, I may at last tell you what you must do."*

"Right," said Stinkbomb. "Well, we'd better get on with it. Come on, Your Majesty."

"Eh? What?" said King Toothbrush Weasel, who hadn't been paying attention.

Just then, a mysterious stranger in a raincoat entered the library. He crossed the room and took a book from one of the shelves. Then there was silence, except for the rumble of the **Number 94 bus** going past outside.

"It's all going very well, isn't it?" said Ketchup-Face happily. "What's the next thing?"

"Next," Stinkbomb reminded her, "it's the end of the chapter."

CHAPTER 7

— · —

IN WHICH
WE FIND PAGE 46, AND OUR HEROES
LEARN WHAT THEY MUST DO

O h, yes," said Ketchup-Face. "So it is. And
the beginning of the next one."

"What was the next thing, again?" Stinkbomb
asked.

"*Let me see,*" said Miss Butterworth, opening
the book again and taking a step toward him.

"**Ow,**" said Malcolm the Cat.

"*Oh, sorry,*" said Miss Butterworth, looking
down and taking her foot off Malcolm the Cat's
tail.

"Yes, that was it," said Stinkbomb.

"And then we can get to **page 46** and you can tell us the secret," said Ketchup-Face.

"But we're only on **page 43**," Stinkbomb pointed out.

So they waited for a bit.

"That's no good," Stinkbomb said eventually. "It's hardly gotten us any closer to **page 46** at all. I suppose we'll have to do something."

"I could sing my song again," Ketchup-Face suggested.

"Yes, all right," agreed Stinkbomb. So Ketchup-Face sang her song again.

"Bother," said Stinkbomb, when she had finished. "That didn't get us much further either."

"I know!" said Ketchup-Face. "I could shout something

REALLY REALLY LOUDLY!"

"GOOD IDEA!"

yelled Stinkbomb, even more loudly.

"*Shhh!*" said Miss Butterworth.

"But it's working!" protested Ketchup-Face.

"Perhaps," Miss Butterworth said, "*but as a Ninja Librarian, I have made vows to preserve the quiet dignity of the library, with exceptions only to be made for Bouncy Sing & Clap Story Time with Miss Tibbles.*"

"Oh," said Stinkbomb. "What would happen if I just went on shouting anyway?"

"*Then,*" Miss Butterworth said sadly, "*I would have to chop your head off with my big sword.*"

Stinkbomb thought about this. The idea of having his head chopped off with Miss Butterworth's big sword certainly sounded interesting, but he wasn't sure if he would actually like it. So he decided to be quieter.

"Well," he said softly, "what are we going to do to get us to **page 46**, then?"

"I know!" said Ketchup-Face. "We could ask that nice Mr. Ricks to draw us a great big picture of a duck-billed platypus."

"That wasn't a duck-billed platypus!" Ketchup-Face said indignantly. "That was a hippotato-mouse!"

"It looked like a duck-billed platypus to me," said King Toothbrush Weasel.

"Never mind that!" said Stinkbomb excitedly. "Look! It's **page 46**! Now Miss Butterworth can tell us how to catch the badgers!"

Miss Butterworth checked the page number, bowed her head in silent agreement, and opened the library's copy of STINKBOMB AND KETCHUP-FACE AND THE QUEST FOR THE MAGIC PORCUPINE to **page 46**.

She scanned the page. *"To catch the badgers,"* she told them, *"you must first fulfill a quest."*

CHAPTER 8

——•——

IN WHICH
OUR HEROES LEARN
OF THEIR QUEST

Let me guess," said Stinkbomb. "Is it a quest for a Magic Porcupine?"

"*It is,*" Miss Butterworth agreed, looking up from the copy of STINKBOMB AND KETCHUP-FACE AND THE QUEST FOR THE MAGIC PORCUPINE.

"I say!" said King Toothbrush Weasel. "However did you know that?"

"*To stop the badgers from doing their evil and wicked doings,*" Miss Butterworth continued, "*you must find the legendary Magic Porcupine of Stupidity.*"

"Stupidity?" asked Ketchup-Face.

"Yes, Stupidity," said Miss Butterworth. *"It's a tiny village where the Magic Porcupine lives."*

"Oh," said Ketchup-Face. "That's a silly name."

"No, it isn't," said King Toothbrush Weasel. "Asillyname is in the other direction."

"Never mind that," said Stinkbomb, who was eager to get on with the story. "How do we get to Stupidity?"

Miss Butterworth thought for a moment, and then she wasn't there anymore.

"How *does* she do that?" asked King Toothbrush Weasel, looking around.

A moment later, just as mysteriously and silently, she returned with another book.

"Ha!" said Malcolm the Cat smugly, twitching his tail out of the way.

King Toothbrush Weasel, curious about the book, edged closer to Miss Butterworth.

"OW!" said Malcolm the Cat.

"Oh, sorry," said King Toothbrush Weasel,

looking down and taking his foot off Malcolm the Cat's tail.

Miss Butterworth held up the book. It was called *Great Destinations for Holidays, Weekend Breaks, and Perilous Quests in Great Kerfuffle*. Turning to the "Perilous Quests" section, she found the entry on Stupidity.

"The road to Stupidity is a long and hard one," she read. *"You must first cross the Valley of Despair—a terrible, desolate place filled with deadly snakes—and then climb the treacherous Mountains of Doom. That done, you must make your way across the dreadful Swamp of Misery, where so many brave adventurers have perished, and if you survive thus far, you must finally face the fiery Volcano of Death, which is also a bit nasty."*

Stinkbomb thought about this. The idea of crossing the Valley of Despair, climbing the Mountains of Doom, making his way across the Swamp of Misery, and facing the Volcano of Death certainly sounded interesting, but he wasn't sure he would actually like it.

"Do we *have* to do all that?" he asked.

"Well," Miss Butterworth said, *"you could take the Number 36 bus instead. It goes the other way, so you wouldn't have to cross the Valley of Despair, climb the Mountains of Doom, make your way across the Swamp of Misery, and face the Volcano of Death, although you would have to endure the Traffic Lights of Waiting a Crazy Long Time."*

"Um . . . I think we'll take the bus," Stinkbomb said, and Ketchup-Face agreed. "Could we have some money for the tickets?" he asked King Toothbrush Weasel.

None of them noticed that, while this conversation was going on, the mysterious stranger in a raincoat had crept closer to them. He was a big mysterious stranger in a raincoat with a big badge that said

Big Mysterious Stranger

As soon as he heard the bit about taking the **Number 36 bus** he turned and hurried out of the library, going as quietly as he could so as not to draw attention to himself, and pausing only to knock over the wastepaper basket.

CHAPTER 9

— · —

IN WHICH
WE VISIT THE LIBRARY ROOF, AND THE CAUSE
OF THE MYSTERIOUS RAIN IS REVEALED

Outside, the mysterious stranger in a rain-coat hurried up the fire escape to the library roof, where he found Harry the Badger and all the other badgers refilling their giant pump-action water guns from a big barrel of extremely dirty river water.

"Hello, Rolf the Badger," said Harry the Badger, pumping his water gun really hard and then **squirting** happily away. All the other Badgers **squirted**, too, covering the village in a horrible, inky-splattery, thick wet rain that left dark splotches on the ground and **smelled** faintly of bananas.

The mysterious stranger in a raincoat took off his raincoat and was indeed Rolf the Badger.

"Hello, Harry the Badger," he said. "What're you doing that for?"

"It's an **evil** and **wicked** doing," Harry the Badger explained.

"Oh, okay," said Rolf the Badger. "Can I have a turn with your water gun?"

Harry the Badger thought about this for a moment. "Nope," he said, squirting some more. "What'd you find out?"

"Well," said Rolf the Badger, "apparently there's this Magic Porcupine in Stupidity that can stop badgers."

"Grrr!" growled Harry the Badger.

"And those kids are going to go on the Number 36 bus and find it."

"Grrrrrrr!" growled Harry the Badger.

"Then they're going to bring it back."

"Grrrrrrrrrrr!"

growled Harry the Badger.

"And then it'll stop us doing our evil and wicked doings."

"Oink!"

growled Harry the Badger. "Sorry, I mean:

Grrrrrrrrrrrrrrrrrrrrrrrrrrrrrr!"

"Now can I have a go with your water gun?"

"No!" said Harry the Badger, putting it down. "We've got to stop those kids from bringing the Magic Porcupine back to Loose Pebbles. How did you say they were getting there?"

"On the **Number 36 bus**," said Rolf the Badger, still eyeing Harry the Badger's water gun enviously.

"Aha!" Harry the Badger said, looking at his watch, and then remembering that he was a badger and didn't have one. "What time is it?"

Rolf the Badger **sniffed** the air and looked at the sky. Animals have senses that we humans don't have, and can find out lots of things by **sniffing** the air and looking at the sky. After a moment, he sniffed again, and said, "Gosh! Did you know that Caracas is the capital of Venezuela?"

"Oooh, is it?" said the other badgers,

and they all began **sniffing** the air and looking at the sky.

"Never mind that!" Harry the Badger snarled. "What *time* is it?"

For a moment there was no sound but the sound of **sniffing** badgers. And then one of them said, "Um . . . it's about five to **Chapter Ten**."

"Perfect!" said Harry the Badger. "The **Number 36 bus** doesn't leave till **Chapter Eleven**. We've just got time! Come on!"

"Hang on a minute," said Rolf the Badger. "I've just realized what that big barrel of river water reminds me of."

And he knocked it over. They watched as its filthy contents poured out and into the street below.

"Hey!" said Harry the Badger. "Who put those banana skins in there?"

CHAPTER 10

—•—

IN WHICH
OUR HEROES SAY GOOD-BYE
TO THEIR FRIENDS

A minute or two later, and an entire library nearer the ground, Stinkbomb and Ketchup-Face stood in the village square saying good-bye to their friends. Or, rather, Ketchup-Face was saying good-bye. Stinkbomb had already said it, like this:

"Bye."

Ketchup-Face, however, had a strong sense of the dramatic, and felt that *bye* didn't quite cover it when you were off on a quest to save the entire kingdom from **evil** and **wickedness.**

"Good-bye, Starlight, my Noble Steed!"

she said to the little shopping cart, trying to throw her arms around it and then giving it a kiss instead.

The little shopping cart blushed. "Good luck," it said shyly.

"And good-bye, Miss Butterworth, protector of the library!" she continued, throwing her arms affectionately around the Ninja Librarian.

Miss Butterworth bowed solemnly. *"Be noble, and strong,"* she said, *"and you will succeed in* your quest. Take this with you." She pressed something into Ketchup-Face's hand. "Use it wisely."

"Thank you!" Ketchup-Face gasped, looking at the small, flat object. "Is it a magic talisman to ward off evil and wickedness?"

"No," said Miss Butterworth. "It is a library card. The mobile library stops in Stupidity most days, and I thought you might like something to read on your way back."

"Oh," said Ketchup-Face. "Thank you." She threw her arms around Malcolm the Cat, gave him a kiss on the nose, and said, "Good-bye, sweet little cat."

Malcolm the Cat stared unblinkingly at her until she began to feel uncomfortable.

Then she turned to King Toothbrush Weasel, and *didn't* throw her arms around him. In fact, she took a step back.

"OW," said Malcolm the Cat.

"Oh, sorry," said Ketchup-Face, looking down and taking her foot off Malcolm the Cat's tail.

Then she looked up at King Toothbrush Weasel. He was dripping wet and **smelled** faintly of bananas, because as he had left the library a few minutes earlier, an enormous raindrop—about the size of a barrelful—had fallen on him.

"Well . . . bye," she said.

"Come on," said Stinkbomb. "The bus'll be going in a minute!"

They both gave a little wave and made their way quickly over to the bus stop where the **Number 36 bus** was sitting, its engine *chugging* away merrily.

CHAPTER 11

—— • ——

IN WHICH
OUR HEROES CATCH THE
NUMBER 36 BUS, AND IT ALMOST LEAVES

"Two children to Stupidity, please!" Stinkbomb said.

"Why, certainly, young gentleman!" said the driver cheerily. "Welcome aboard! I'm Mr. Jolly, the bus driver! Can I check that it *is* the **Number 36** you want, and not the **36A**?"

"Er ... what's the difference?" asked Stinkbomb.

"Well," said Mr. Jolly with a jovial wink, "they both go to Stupidity, but the **Number 36A** takes the scenic route through the Valley of Despair, over the Mountains of Doom, across the Swamp

of Misery, and past the Volcano of Death, while the **36**—that's this one—goes the direct route via the Traffic Lights of Waiting a Crazy Long Time."

"Oh, okay," said Stinkbomb. "Yes, it's definitely the **36** we want."

"Righty-ho," said Mr. Jolly, a merry twinkle in his eye. "Very wise, if you ask me. I probably shouldn't say this, but Mr. Creepy, who drives the **36A**, he's a bit . . . well . . ."

"Creepy?" suggested Ketchup-Face.

"Oh, no!" said Mr. Jolly in surprise. "No, I

wouldn't say that. I was going to say 'nervous.' What made you think he'd be creepy?"

"Well," said Ketchup-Face slowly, "you're called Mr. Jolly . . ."

"That I am!" agreed Mr. Jolly happily.

". . . and you *are* jolly."

"That's true!" Mr. Jolly exclaimed. "That's a very good point indeed!"

"So I just thought," Ketchup-Face continued, "that if a bus driver called Mr. Jolly *is* jolly, then maybe a bus driver called Mr. Creepy would be creepy."

Mr. Jolly sat back in his seat and scratched his chin. "I never thought of that!" he said. "Fancy me being so jolly when my name *is* Jolly! What a coincidence, eh? And now that I think about it," he added confidentially, "there *is* something creepy about Mr. Creepy." He scratched his chin some more. "And he's not really nervous at all. I was mixing him up with the chap who drives the **Number 35A**. What's his name again? Oh, yes: Mr. Nervous." A look of delighted surprise came over his face. "And come to think of it—he *is* nervous! Deary me!" And he burst into a **guffaw** of hearty laughter that shook the whole bus. "Well," he said, wiping the tears of merriment from his eyes and looking at his watch, "better get going. It's nearly the end of the **chapter**. Take your seats, young lady and young gentleman."

He was just putting the bus into gear when, from outside, there came a great shout of,

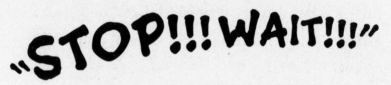

"**STOP!!! WAIT!!!**"

And they turned to see a crowd of raccoons racing across the square toward them.

CHAPTER 12

——•——

IN WHICH
SOME RACCOONS CATCH
THE NUMBER 36 BUS

As the bus doors **hissed** open again, the raccoons swarmed aboard.

"Lots of raccoons to Stupidity, please," said one of the raccoons.

"How many raccoons, exactly?" asked Mr. Jolly. The raccoons looked at one another, and shrugged. "Dunno," one of them said. "We don't do math. We're raccoons."

Mr. Jolly beamed. "Well, young Master Raccoon," he said, "how's about you give me fifty cents each, then? Be quick about it—we're running late! We should have left over a page ago."

There was a lot of scuffling and mumbling about change, but finally the raccoons all had their tickets and took their seats, and the bus was on its way.

Everyone was very excited to be on the bus—especially Stinkbomb and Ketchup-Face, who had never been on a bus by themselves before

because it was the sort of thing they were only allowed to do in stories.

It wasn't long, though, before Stinkbomb began to grow suspicious.

"You know," he murmured to his sister, "there's something odd about those raccoons."

"Really?" whispered Ketchup-Face. "Do you think maybe they're not raccoons at all?"

"It's possible," Stinkbomb said.

"Shall we find out?"

"Okay," said Stinkbomb, "but we'll have to be clever about it. We don't want them to know that we suspect anything."

Ketchup-Face nodded wisely. "Leave it to me," she told him, and she turned around and said to the raccoon in the seat behind her, "Excuse me, but are you *really* raccoons?"

The raccoon jumped guiltily. "Oh, yes," it said. "We're definitely raccoons. We're very raccoony indeed. Never been raccoonier. Isn't that right, Rolf the Raccoon?"

"That's right," agreed Rolf the Raccoon, a big raccoon with a big badge that said  "We're raccoons all right. Aren't we, Harry the Raccoon?"

"Yes," agreed Harry the Raccoon, taking a sip of tea from a mug marked "We're extremely raccoony. Aren't we, Stewart the Raccoon?"

Just as Stewart the Raccoon was opening his

mouth to answer, Harry the Raccoon passed him
a note that said:

Pretend we're raccoons.

Stewart the Raccoon read it slowly three times
and then said, "Er, we're raccoons." He turned the
note over. On the other side, it said:

Don't let them know we're badgers.

"Er, we're not badgers," he added.

"Oh, good," said Ketchup-Face, reassured.

But Stinkbomb was still suspicious. **"Aren't raccoons supposed to have long, ringed tails?"** he asked.

"We *do* have long, ringed tails," said Harry the Raccoon. "Look!" And he opened a bag he was carrying and let Stinkbomb and Ketchup-Face look inside. It was full of long, ringed tails.

"Aren't those supposed to be on your bottoms?" asked Ketchup-Face curiously.

"Not when you're running for a bus," said Harry the Raccoon. "You might trip over them."

Ketchup-Face nodded wisely, but Stinkbomb was still not satisfied. "Are you *absolutely* sure you're raccoons?" he said.

"Absolutely," said Harry the Raccoon. "We've even got **black masks** on our faces."

"Yes . . . but they seem to be held on with elastic," said Stinkbomb thoughtfully.

"So?" said Harry the Raccoon rudely, but not too rudely, because he didn't want anyone to realize he was really a bad guy.

Just then, Ketchup-Face pointed out of the window, and said, "What's that?"

Stinkbomb looked. "It's the river," he said. "You know, the River Yuk. The big one that flows all the way from Stupidity to Loose Pebbles."

"What's it for?" Ketchup-Face asked.

"I don't think it's *for* anything," Stinkbomb said. "Though if it was cleaner I suppose you could swim in it, or fish in it."

"And you could fill barrels from it," suggested Stewart the Raccoon.

All the other raccoons glared at him and made **shushing** signs with their eyebrows.

"Er . . . if you wanted to," Stewart the Raccoon added. "But I don't want to. I don't like barrels. Or garbage cans. I'm a raccoon."

Then there was silence on the bus, as it trundled on toward Stupidity.

And then they reached the Traffic Lights of Waiting a Crazy Long Time.

CHAPTER 13

IN WHICH
WE WAIT FOR A RATHER LONG TIME
AT THE TRAFFIC LIGHTS OF WAITING A CRAZY LONG TIME

R ight," said Mr. Jolly in a slightly less jolly voice. "This is where we wait for a crazy long time."

And they did.

CHAPTER 14

IN WHICH
WE ARE STILL WAITING AT THE
TRAFFIC LIGHTS OF WAITING A CRAZY LONG TIME

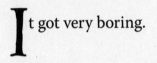

It got very boring.

CHAPTER 15

— • —

IN WHICH
WE ARE STILL WAITING
AT THE TRAFFIC LIGHTS OF
WAITING A CRAZY LONG TIME

Very, very boring.

CHAPTERS 16,
17, 18, 19, 20, 21, 22,
23, 24, 25, 26, 27, 28,
29, 30, 31, 32, 33, 34,
35, 36, 37, 38, 39, 40, 41,
42, 43, 44, 45, 46 AND 47

— · —

IN WHICH
WE SAVE PAPER BY HAVING
ALL THE REST OF THE CHAPTERS
INVOLVING WAITING AT THE TRAFFIC LIGHTS
OF WAITING A CRAZY LONG TIME ON THE SAME PAGE

They went on waiting...

and nothing...

interesting...

happened.

CHAPTER 48

---•---

IN WHICH,
QUITE UNEXPECTEDLY, THERE IS A BIT
MORE WAITING AT THE TRAFFIC LIGHTS
OF WAITING A CRAZY LONG TIME

Surely the light should have changed by now!" Stinkbomb grumbled. He was beginning to wish they had gone the other way and crossed the Valley of Despair, climbed the Mountains of Doom, made their way across the Swamp of Misery, and faced the Volcano of Death instead.

He was sure it would have been more interesting.

Ketchup-Face jumped up and pointed toward the big window at

the back of the bus. "Look!" she cried. "It's the mobile library."

She waved at the nice lady who was driving the mobile library, and the nice lady waved back. It was Miss Tibbles, who ran Bouncy Sing & Clap Story Time for toddlers at the main library.

Ketchup-Face waved again, and so did Stinkbomb, and Miss Tibbles waved back again, and made a funny face. The raccoons joined in too. A few of them got very excited and began to be a bit silly, and some of them even showed Miss Tibbles their long, ringed tails and waggled

them about, which sounds rude until you remember that their tails were in a bag and not on their bottoms.

And so they kept themselves amused while they waited for the light to change.

CHAPTER 49

—— · ——

IN WHICH,
AT LAST, THE LIGHT CHANGES
AND THE BUS CONTINUES ON

At last, the light changed and the bus continued on. And Stinkbomb and Ketchup-Face and the raccoons went on waving and making faces at Miss Tibbles until the **rocking** of the bus made them sleepy, and one by one they all sat back in their seats and dozed off.

CHAPTER 50

—•—

IN WHICH
THE BUS FINALLY REACHES
STUPIDITY

The bus shuddered to a halt. From all around came the sound of raccoons yawning and stretching.

"*Eeeek!*" squeaked Stewart the Raccoon, as he opened his eyes. "*We're surrounded by bandits!*"

Harry the Raccoon clipped him around the ear. "That's not bandits," he said gruffly. "That's our reflections in the windows."

"Lady and gentleman and raccoons, welcome to Stupidity!" said Mr. Jolly.

The bus door opened with a **hiss**—and

everyone froze in horror. There, right at the foot of the steps, was a deadly snake. It raised its hooded head, displaying its lethal fangs. Its little beadlike eyes glittered; its gaze swept over them all before fixing on Mr. Jolly.

"Excuse me," it said, "but does this bus go to the Valley of Despair?"

"No," said Mr. Jolly cheerily, "that's the **36A** you'll be wanting, young Master Deadly Snake. It should be along in a bit."

"Oh, thanks," said the deadly snake happily. "I was afraid I was going to be late for dinner again."

"I probably shouldn't say this," Mr. Jolly added, as the deadly snake **slithered** back a little to let Stinkbomb, Ketchup-Face, and the raccoons off the bus, "but watch out for Mr. Creepy, the driver. He's a bit . . . well . . ."

"Creepy?" suggested the deadly snake.

"Oh, no!" said Mr. Jolly in surprise. "No, I wouldn't say that at all. I was going to say 'short-tempered.'" He paused, and scratched his chin. "Or maybe I'm getting him mixed up with the man who drives the **Number 33**. Now, what's his name again . . . ?"

"Okay," said Stinkbomb, as he and Ketchup-Face and the raccoons made their way across the little village square, "where's this Magic Porcupine?"

Stupidity was a tiny little village. Aside from the bus stop there was nothing in it except two houses stuck together, and a mud hut. There was no shop; there was no movie theater; there was no post office; there was no restaurant; there wasn't even a nuclear research facility or a space shuttle launchpad.

There was, however, a mobile library, which had just pulled up in the middle of the village square. As Miss Tibbles opened the doors, Stewart the Raccoon raced excitedly across to it.

"Excuse me," he said. "Can I have an ice cream sandwich, please?"

Miss Tibbles smiled. "No, my lovely," she said kindly. "This isn't an ice cream truck; it's a mobile library."

"Oh," said Stewart the Raccoon sadly.

"I know," said Stinkbomb. "Let's ask Miss Tibbles."

"Hello, you two," Miss Tibbles greeted them. "Aren't your parents with you today?"

"Oh, no," said Ketchup-Face. "They like to stay out of the way when we're in a story."

Miss Tibbles went a bit pink. "Are we in a story?" she said. "Oh, dear. Does my hair look all right?"

"It looks really nice," Stinkbomb assured her. "Do you know anything about the Magic Porcupine?"

"Oh, yes," Miss Tibbles said. "It's quite lovely, the Magic Porcupine. And it's very, very magical. It can do the most amazing things. Why do you ask?"

"Well," said Stinkbomb, "the badgers have escaped from prison, and the only one who can foil their evil and wicked plans is the Magic Porcupine, so we're on a quest to find it."

"And, er, we'd like to see it do some magic," added Harry the Raccoon, who—along with all the other raccoons—had come over to join them.

Miss Tibbles nodded wisely. "Well," she said, "you might try that mud hut over there. That's where it lives."

"Oh," said Ketchup-Face. "Thanks."

CHAPTER 51

—— • ——

IN WHICH
OUR HEROES MEET
THE MAGIC PORCUPINE
OF STUPIDITY

The mud hut was dark inside, and dimly lit by candles. Black shadows on the walls danced a strange and eerie dance, like your granny at Christmas when she's had too much fizzy wine.

Ketchup-Face edged closer to Stinkbomb and took his hand. "It will be a *nice* Magic Porcupine, won't it?"

"Dunno," said Stinkbomb. He was secretly hoping the

Magic Porcupine would be like a grumpy old wizard with lightning flashing from his staff and a habit of saying "Bah!" a lot.

Suddenly, the candles **flamed** and **flared** wildly, and a figure stepped from the shadows.

It was the Magic Porcupine of Stupidity.

"Oooooooh,"

went all the raccoons excitedly.

It was hard to see the Magic Porcupine clearly in the dimness and gloom of the hut, but

Stinkbomb and Ketchup-Face could make out the shape of the long, sharp quills that covered its body, and the **tall** wizardy hat on its head. The whole effect was terrifically mysterious, and very exciting, and *extremely* magical.

"Um . . . hello, everybody," said the Magic Porcupine. "Would you like to see some magic?"

"Oooh, yes please!"

said all the raccoons.

Stinkbomb hugged himself excitedly. "Maybe it'll conjure lightning from the skies!" he whispered to his sister. "Or make the whole hut fly up into the air! Or make a fountain of gold coins spring up from the earth!"

"Or turn a prince into a handsome frog!" Ketchup-Face suggested.

"Right, then," said the Magic Porcupine. "Pick a card—any card."

"Um . . . this one!" said Harry the Raccoon.

"Look at it, and put it back in the pack," said the Magic Porcupine. "And . . . is *this* your card?" It plucked the ten of diamonds from the top of the pack and held it up triumphantly.

Harry the Raccoon shrugged. "Can't remember," he said. "I think mine was that sort of color, though."

"It was definitely that shape," added Stewart the Raccoon helpfully.

The Magic Porcupine sagged a little. "Oh well," it said. "Let's try something else, then. Erm . . .

Abracadabra!"

It reached forward and plucked a small coin from behind Ketchup-Face's ear.

"Oooh," said all the raccoons politely, and they clapped.

But Stinkbomb was not so easily impressed. "There's something funny about this," he said. "We need a better look at this Magic Porcupine. Where's the light switch?"

Ketchup-Face peered into the gloom. "I don't think there is one," she said.

"Oh," said Stinkbomb. "Well . . . hang on, I think I've got one in my pocket."

Sure enough, a quick fumble in his pocket produced a square, white plastic light switch.

"Right," he said. "Ready?"

Ketchup-Face nodded. Stinkbomb pressed the switch.

The mud hut was

flooded

with

light.

CHAPTER 52

— • —

IN WHICH
SECRETS ARE REVEALED

The Magic Porcupine was magically producing a bunch of flowers out of thin air. But as the lights blazed on, everyone could see that it was actually whipping them out from underneath its tall wizardy hat.

"Oh, dear!" said the Magic Porcupine, trying to stuff the flowers back under its hat so quickly that the hat fell off, revealing a pair of **tall** floppy ears.

"You're not doing real magic at all!" said Stinkbomb.

"And I don't think you're even a proper porcu-pine!" added Ketchup-Face.

"I am!" said the Magic Porcupine unconvinc-ingly.

"Then why have you got a zipper up your front?" asked Stinkbomb.

"And why do you have such **tall** floppy ears?" added Ketchup-Face.

"Yeah!" said Stinkbomb. "You're not a Magic Porcupine at all—you're just a rabbit in a **spiky** coat!"

The Magic Porcupine's face crumpled. It pulled a hankie from the sleeve of its **spiky** coat and blew its nose into it. "You're right," it admitted. "I'm not the Magic Porcupine."

"Why were you trying to trick us, you naughty rab-bit?" demanded Ketchup-Face.

The rabbit burst into tears.

Ketchup-Face felt immediately sorry. "Oh, please don't be sad," she said.

"Yes," said Stinkbomb, who was equally kind at heart. "I'm sure you didn't mean to be naughty. You seem like a very nice rabbit."

The rabbit sniffled again, and dried its eyes. "I'm sorry," it said. "It's just that—well, this arrived this morning."

It handed them a crumpled note:

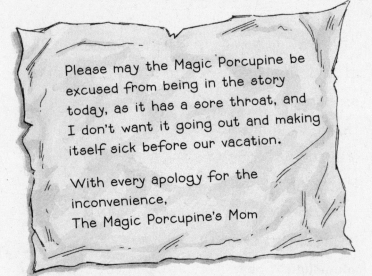

Please may the Magic Porcupine be excused from being in the story today, as it has a sore throat, and I don't want it going out and making itself sick before our vacation.

With every apology for the inconvenience,
The Magic Porcupine's Mom

"So you see," said the rabbit, "we needed another Magic Porcupine, or the story would just have stopped in the middle of **Chapter Fifty-One** without a proper ending or anything."

"But why didn't they just get another Magic Porcupine?" said Stinkbomb.

The rabbit sighed. "There aren't many really magical animals. And most of them already have jobs in those books about the boy who goes to wizarding school. So they asked me, because last week I borrowed a book about magic from Miss Tibbles. I've been practicing really hard."

"But you don't have any *real* magic?" asked Ketchup-Face.

"No," admitted the rabbit sadly.

"But that means you won't be able to do any magic on the badgers," said Stinkbomb. "And that means you won't be able to defeat them and put an end to their **evil** and **wicked** doings."

"And *that* means," put in Harry the Raccoon, "that we don't need our disguises!"

And with a **twang** of elastic, all the raccoons took off their **black masks**, revealing them-selves to be none other than . . .

the badgers!

"Gosh," said Stinkbomb. "That was unexpected."

"So Harry the Raccoon was really Harry the Badger all the time!" Ketchup-Face gasped. "And Rolf the Raccoon was really Rolf the Badger, and Stewart the Raccoon was really Stewart the Badger!"

"Ah! Ah ha ha ha ha ha!"

chuckled Harry the Raccoon. "That's what was so clever about our **evil** and **wicked** plan!" He straightened up and put on a big badge that said BIG BADGER. "We fooled you completely! I am actually Rolf the Badger!"

"Yeah," said Rolf the Raccoon, stepping down off the **tall** platform shoes that nobody had noticed he was wearing, and taking off the coat that was exactly like his own fur, only bulkier and with a big badge that said **BIG RACCOON** pinned to it. "And I'm really Harry the Badger. So there."

Everybody looked at Stewart the Raccoon, who just shrugged and shuffled his paws and said in a small voice, "Nobody wanted to swap with me . . ."

"Anyway," said Harry the Badger, "with the Magic Porcupine out of the way, nothing can stop us doing some **evil** and **wicked** doings!"

"*We* can!" said Stinkbomb bravely.

"Oh, yeah?" said Harry the Badger. "Well, not if we tie you up and throw you in the river!"

And they tied them up and threw them in the river.

CHAPTER 53

—— • ——

IN WHICH
THE BADGERS MAKE THEIR GETAWAY, AND OUR HEROES FIND THEMSELVES IN
TERRIBLE DANGER

HeLP!" shouted Ketchup-Face.

"Glub!" said the rabbit, getting a face full of dirty river water.

"Why aren't we sinking?" asked Stinkbomb, being a practical sort of child. "I thought the badgers tied us up before they threw us in the river."

"That's right," agreed Harry the Badger from the steep bank above them. "We tied you up with really strong rope, didn't we, Rolf the Badger?"

"Yes," agreed Rolf the Badger. "Well, sort of. But we didn't use proper knots. That'd be dangerous. We may be the bad guys, but we're not *that* bad."

"I wish we weren't the bad guys at all," said Stewart the Badger sadly. "I'd like to be a good guy for a change."

"I know!" said Harry the Badger. "Let's catch the bus back to Loose Pebbles and get rid of King Toothbrush Weasel! Then maybe in the next story, with all the good guys out of the way, *we'll* get to be the good guys!"

"Does it work like that?" asked Stewart the Badger cautiously.

Harry the Badger shrugged. "Dunno," he said. "But it's worth a try. Look—here comes the bus now!"

Sure enough, a bus was just pulling in to the village square. Displayed on the front were the words

LOOSE PEBBLES

written in big letters. Below that, in smaller letters, it said

via the Volcano of Death, the Swamp
of Misery, the Mountains of Doom, and
the Valley of Despair

It was the **Number 36A**, and it was driven
by a man who looked . . . well, a bit creepy, really.

"Quick!" said Harry the Badger.

The badgers all rushed across the square and
scrambled on board, pushing past the deadly
snake. Moments later, in a cloud of dust, the bus
was gone.

"What do we do now?" asked Stinkbomb,
treading water.

"Oh," said Ketchup-Face breezily, "something's
bound to turn up."

"**Eeek!**" said the rabbit.

"What do you mean, *Eeek!*?" Ketchup-Face
demanded.

"**Eeeeek!**" explained the rabbit, pointing
with a trembling foot.

Stinkbomb and Ketchup-Face turned, and

froze with horror. There, cutting through the water toward them with terrifying speed, was a sinister gray triangular fin.

"Eeek!" agreed Ketchup-Face.

"It's a SHARK!"

The shark began to circle them, drawing closer with each turn. Stinkbomb and Ketchup-Face, still treading water, clutched each other for comfort, letting out little whimpers of fear as the huge creature brushed their legs.

And then the shark spoke. Its voice came up from the water, a menacing **rumble** that chilled their blood.

"I am hungry!"

CHAPTER 54

—— • ——

IN WHICH
YOU HAVE TO READ THE CHAPTER TO FIND OUT
WHETHER OR NOT OUR HEROES GET
EATEN BY A SHARK

Eeeek!" said the rabbit again. "We're going to get eaten!"

The shark circled menacingly, displaying a cruel mouth full of jagged triangular teeth. Angling away from them, it turned and made a sudden dash back.

"I am hungry!" it **rumbled** again, butting Stinkbomb's legs with its wide flat head. "I don't suppose you've got any bananas?"

"Bananas?" squeaked the rabbit.

Ketchup-Face said nothing, but suddenly looked slightly smug.

Stinkbomb eyed the shark more carefully. "You're a hammerhead shark, aren't you?" he said.

"Yeah!" said the shark in surprise, raising one eye out of the water to look at him. "How'd you know that?"

"Well," said Stinkbomb, "your head's shaped like a hammer."

The shark thought about this. **"Ohhhhh,"** it said. "Hammer . . . head. Head like a hammer. That makes sense. Funny I never realized before. So . . . *do* you have any bananas?"

"Um . . . I think I might, actually," Stinkbomb said, fumbling in his pocket and producing a small bunch.

"Thanks," said the shark. It neatly snipped off the ends of the bananas with its teeth and **sucked** the fruit out,

leaving Stinkbomb holding the empty skins. "Yum," it said.

"I didn't think hammerhead sharks ate bananas," said the rabbit. "Not that I'm complaining," it added quickly. "Eat as many bananas as you like. I bet they're much tastier than rabbits and children. I just didn't think you *did* eat bananas, that's all."

"Me neither," Stinkbomb agreed. "I thought you were a bottom feeder."

"**Ewwww,**" said the shark. "That sounds disgusting."

"I mean," explained Stinkbomb quickly, "I thought you ate things off the bottom of the sea."

"Oh, yes," agreed the shark. "I do that, all right. That's how I found out about bananas. I was swimming along one day, when a sailor holding a bunch of bananas fell out of a boat and landed on the seabed. So I ate them. And they were delicious, too. The bananas, that is. I don't eat sailors. I gave him a ride home instead."

"Where does he live?" asked Ketchup-Face.

"Here, on Great Kerfuffle," said the shark. "Down the river, in Asillyname. Which is funny, 'cause he actually has a silly name. He's called Captain Bonkers."

"That *is* a silly name," agreed Ketchup-Face.

"I stayed in the river," the shark went on, "just swimming up and down, 'cause he's been bringing me bananas and they're so tasty. But I haven't seen him since Tuesday, and I've been getting a bit hungry."

"What do you do with the skins?" Stinkbomb asked.

"Oh, I just drop them on the riverbed," the shark said. "I've been dropping them in a neat little pile under the bridge at Loose Pebbles. This morning some badgers came along with a barrel and fished them out."

"The badgers!" said Stinkbomb, his suspicions instantly aroused and his clever brain starting to put things together. "Did they fish out anything else?"

"Just some water and mud," the shark said.

"Was it the sort of mud that would make water horrible, inky-splattery, thick, wet, and darkly splotchy?" asked Stinkbomb.

The shark shrugged, which is difficult for something with no shoulders. "I suppose it would," it said.

"And the banana skins would make it **smell** faintly of bananas!" said Ketchup-Face.

"Exactly!" said Stinkbomb. "But that doesn't help us stop them. We'll never get back to Loose Pebbles in time."

"You might," suggested the shark. "If I give you a ride. Hop on!"

"Thanks!" said Stinkbomb, scrambling onto the shark's back.

"Yes, thanks!" said the rabbit, clambering up behind him.

"GIDDYUP!"

said Ketchup-Face, climbing on in front.

CHAPTER 55

—— · ——

IN WHICH
OUR HEROES GO ON AN EXCITING
SHARKBACK RIDE IN A BRAVE ATTEMPT
TO SAVE THE DAY

Traveling on sharkback was gloriously exciting. It was even faster than the little shopping cart, and it didn't keep veering off to the left or leave a crisscross pattern on your bottom. On they sped, leaving behind them a great trail of white, frothing, foaming water that **smelled** very, very faintly of bananas.

"What did you say your names were again?" asked the shark.

"Stinkbomb," said Stinkbomb.

"Ketchup-Face," said Ketchup-Face.

"The legendary Magic Porcupine of Stupidity," said the rabbit.

"Really?" said the hammerhead shark. "You look more like a rabbit in a **spiky** coat to me."

The rabbit looked a little crestfallen. "I'm just the stand-in," it admitted.

"And what's your name?" asked Stinkbomb. He was already looking forward to telling his friends all about his death-defying ride on the back of a shark, and thought it would be even more exciting if he could tell them that the shark was called

Killer, or
Daggerteeth,
or Terror of the Deep.

"Felicity," said the shark.

"Oh," said Stinkbomb. "Is that short for anything?" he added hopefully. "Like Felicity the Devourer of Thousands, or Felicity the Great Death-Machine of the Ocean?"

"Nope," said the shark happily. "Just Felicity. I did have an uncle once who was called Arthur the Devourer of **Hundreds** and **Thousands**, but that was because he liked those little colorful bobbly bits they sometimes put on ice cream. Any time you had an ice cream, Uncle Arthur would come along and devour the **hundreds** and **thousands** before you had a chance to." Felicity sighed. "Poor old Uncle Arthur. It was sad, what happened to him."

"Oh," said Stinkbomb. "What did happen?"

The shark sighed again. "All his teeth went rotten and fell out. Apparently those things are pure sugar. Now they call him Arthur the Devourer of **Soup** and **Soggy Cereal**. It's a pretty bad name, really."

"Yes, it is," said Stinkbomb, thinking himself lucky he wasn't stuck with a silly name.

"Oh, dear," said the rabbit, **sniffing** the air and looking at the sky. "It's getting late. I hope we can stop the badgers before the end of the story."

"We will," said Ketchup-Face confidently. "It's that kind of story."

"Besides," added Stinkbomb, "Felicity's going faster than the **36A**, and that goes the long way around. We'll get to Loose Pebbles in plenty of time to warn everybody."

But what Stinkbomb had no way of knowing was that the **36A** was no longer going the long way around. It had come to a sign that said:

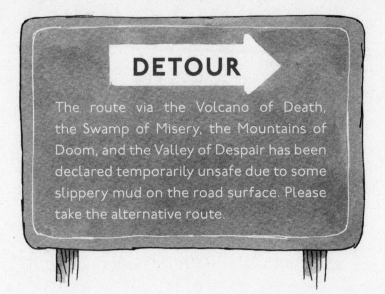

DETOUR →

The route via the Volcano of Death, the Swamp of Misery, the Mountains of Doom, and the Valley of Despair has been declared temporarily unsafe due to some slippery mud on the road surface. Please take the alternative route.

Not only that, but Mr. Creepy had made the mistake of stopping the bus and getting off to use the toilet, and of course the badgers had immediately stolen it—the bus, that is, not the toilet. Now they were driving it too fast toward the unsuspecting village of Loose Pebbles.

And there was no one there to warn the villagers of the avalanche of badgery badness that was about to sweep down over them.

CHAPTER 56

---•---

IN WHICH
THE BADGERS DRIVE
TOO FAST

The animals that lived near the bank of the River Yuk **sniffed** the air, and looked at the sky, and glanced at each other worriedly.

"Can it be . . . ?" whispered an old mole.

"Surely not," muttered a toad.

"Could we be mistaken?" asked a water rat; and they all **sniffed** the air and looked at the sky again.

"It's true, all right," said a squirrel sadly. "There really is a one-in-seventy-million chance of any of us being killed or injured by an asteroid during our lifetime."

"We weren't talking about that," said the water rat impatiently. "Anyway, one-in-seventy-million means hardly any chance at all."

"You've more chance of winning the lottery," agreed a hedgehog.

"Or getting struck by lightning," added a thrush.

"Really?" said the squirrel, and it rushed off to buy a lottery ticket and a pair of rubber boots.

The other animals shook their heads sadly, and sniffed the air and looked at the sky again.

"It's true," said the old mole. "Those wicked badgers have stolen Mr. Creepy's bus and are driving it too fast toward Loose Pebbles."

"And here they come now!" said the water rat.

As the **Number 36A bus** roared past, chock-full of badgers and trailing a huge filthy cloud of dust and fumes behind it, the creatures angrily made their displeasure clear. The mole

booed, the toad **hissed**, the water rat **shouted** a naughty word, the hedgehog performed a short but powerful piece of theater, and the thrush got out a catapult and a bag of snails. A blackbird **blew a raspberry**, a raspbird **blacked a blueberry**, a bluebird **rasped a blackberry**, and in the river a school of minnows quickly made some banners and organized a demonstration.

But all for nothing. The badgers drove on, their attention focused only on their **wicked** and **evil** plans, on driving too fast, and on trying to find a

radio station
that was play-
ing music they all
liked.

As the bus disappeared
into the distance, the squirrel
returned, **sniffing** the air and looking at the sky.

"All is not lost!" it said, carefully
tucking its lottery ticket into one of its
rubber boots. "Two children and a Magic
Porcupine are coming down the river on
the back of a hammerhead shark to save
the day!"

"Now you're just being silly," grumbled
the water rat.

But even as it spoke, a magnificent sight appeared upstream. Felicity was swimming faster than ever, her mighty tail driving her powerfully onward. On her back rode three heroic figures, like warriors of old only smaller and, in the case of the one at the front, rather more ketchup-stained. It was so completely splendid and awe-inspiring that suddenly and out of nowhere an invisible orchestra began to play a majestic and stirring theme tune.

The animals began to cheer, and the minnows quickly changed their banners to read *"Hooray!"* instead of *"Boo!"*

Stinkbomb waved proudly. Ketchup-Face stood up to take a bow, and fell off into the river with a big splash, so Felicity had to stop to let her get back on again.

And then the water rat shouted, "Wait a minute! That's not a Magic Porcupine! It's a rabbit in a **spiky** coat!".

"Humph," grumped the other animals. And they all sloped off angrily, while the dramatic theme music ended in a **discordant clanging** as all the invisible musicians fell off their chairs.

"I may be just a rabbit in a **spiky** coat," shouted the rabbit unhappily, standing up and shaking its paws at them, "but I'm the only Magic Porcupine you've got!"

But the riverbank animals had left.

CHAPTER 57

— • —

IN WHICH
THE RABBIT IN THE SPIKY COAT IS SAD

BOO-HOO," sobbed the rabbit.

"Oh, don't cry, sweet little rabbit!" said Ketchup-Face earnestly, and she stood up and threw her arms around it. **"OW!"** she added, after pricking her fingers on its spiky coat.

This made the rabbit cry even more. "It's no use!" it said. "This story needs a *proper* Magic Porcupine.

The badgers are going to win, and we'll have to spend the rest of our lives sitting on a shark!"

Stinkbomb thought about this. The idea of spending the rest of his life sitting on a shark certainly sounded interesting, but he wasn't sure he would actually like it. So he decided to cheer the rabbit up.

"This story *does* need a Magic Porcupine," he said. "And you're right—you're the only Magic Porcupine we've got! We need you!"

"But all I can do are silly conjuring tricks," the rabbit said, pulling a large spotted hankie from behind Stinkbomb's ear and blowing its nose on it—the hankie, that is, not the ear. "How can I possibly help defeat the badgers?"

"I think I know!" Stinkbomb said. "I've just thought of a Clever Plan!"

"Tell us on the way," suggested Felicity, **sniffing** the air and looking at the sky. "The badgers are going to reach Loose Pebbles ahead of us after all!"

"WHEEE!" shouted Ketchup-Face, as Felicity's tail thrashed the river once more, and they took off like a mighty fish-powered rocket.

"Giddyup Fishy!"

CHAPTER 58

—•—

IN WHICH
OUR HEROES NEAR THE VILLAGE,
AND THE STORY NEARS THE END

Mr. and Mrs. Neck and their children, Samuel and Philippa, were out for a bicycle ride by the river when suddenly a hammerhead shark pulled up beside them and the little girl on its back asked, "Excuse me, have you seen some badgers driving a bus too fast?"

"Yes, we have!" said Mrs. Neck. "Not very long ago, actually. We'd stopped to say 'Good evening' to King Toothbrush Weasel . . ."

"And suddenly a bus full of badgers roared

around the corner going much too fast," added Mr. Neck.

"Yes," said Samuel. "They stopped, and tied up King Toothbrush Weasel and threw him in the bus and drove off too fast again."

"You know," said Philippa, "I think there was something suspicious about that. Should we tell someone?"

"No need!" said Stinkbomb importantly. "I am Stinkbomb, and this is Ketchup-Face, and we have gone on a quest to Stupidity and brought back a Magic Porcupine to take care of the badgers and rescue King Toothbrush Weasel!"

"That's not a Magic Porcupine," said Samuel. "It's a rabbit in a **spiky** coat."

The rabbit folded its paws crossly.

"Did the badgers say where they were going?" Ketchup-Face asked.

"No," said Mr. Neck, "they didn't."

"Although, just before they drove off," said Philippa, "they changed the display on the front of the bus. Instead of saying

LOOSE PEBBLES

— ·· —

via the Volcano of Death, the Swamp
of Misery, the Mountains of Doom,
and the Valley of Despair

it said

THE OLD DESERTED WAREHOUSE
--- --- ---
Next To The River

Does that help?"

"Yes!" said Stinkbomb. "It does! Thanks!"

"Giddyup, fishy!" added Ketchup-Face.

And with a mighty thrashing of a sharky tail, they were gone.

The Neck family watched them go.

"Do you know," said Mr. Neck, "I wonder if perhaps those badgers have kidnapped King Toothbrush Weasel."

"I was just thinking the same thing," said Mrs. Neck. "I wonder where they've taken him?"

"Hmmm," said Samuel. "You know, if I were a bad guy, and I'd kidnapped someone and wanted to hide him, I'd probably take him somewhere not many people go. Like . . ."

"Like the old deserted warehouse next to the river?" suggested Philippa.

CHAPTER 59

——— · ———

IN WHICH
THE STORY RACES TOWARD AN EXCITING CLIMAX

The old deserted warehouse next to the river was very old, and completely deserted. It was also a warehouse. And it was next to the river, which meant that Felicity was able to take them almost to the door.

"Good luck," she whispered.

"Thanks," Stinkbomb and Ketchup-Face whispered back, and, along with the rabbit, they leapt onto the riverbank and crept past the abandoned **Number 36A bus**, and then up to the entrance.

"Right," whispered Stinkbomb. "Here's the

plan. We'll sneak in, and rescue King Toothbrush Weasel, and sneak out again. If we see any badgers, it's Clever Plan time. But we probably won't meet anybody, because it's an old deserted warehouse, so it's deserted." Quietly, he turned the handle and pushed the door.

All the people inside who were standing near the door moved out of the way to let them in.

"Hello!" said Mr. Neck. "After we talked to you, we thought we ought to tell some other people as well, and it turned out that everyone in the village wanted to come and help."

"Then why aren't you helping?" asked Ketchup-Face.

"Oh . . . Well," said Mrs. Neck, "it actually looks rather interesting, and everyone's decided to see what happens."

It did look interesting. At the far end of the vast room, the badgers had built a stage, and across the stage was a large curtain.

"Well," said Ketchup-Face, "I don't care how

interesting it is. If those badgers are doing it, it's probably an **evil** and **wicked** doing. 'Scuse us! Magic Porcupine coming through!"

"That's not a Magic Porcupine," complained somebody. "It's a rabbit in a **spiky** coat!"

The rabbit ignored him.

Just then, the badgers appeared onstage.

"Ladies and gentlemen!" announced Harry the Badger. "Welcome to the end of the story! I know that most of you was probably expectin' an ending in which we all get caught and sent back to prison, but that'd be boring . . ."

"For us," put in Rolf the Badger.

"Yeah," agreed Harry the Badger. "So we've thought up a much more excitin' and interestin' ending."

He pulled back the curtain, and everyone gasped; for there, tied to an enormous water rocket, was King Toothbrush Weasel.

"Blimey O'Reilly!" said Blimey O'Reilly.

"Gordon Bennett!" said Gordon Bennett.

"My goodness!" said Maya Goodness.

"Flippin' 'eck!" said Phillippa Neck.

"Oh dear!" said a roe deer.

"How did that deer get in here?" asked an elephant; but everyone ignored it.

"Stinkbomb," whispered Ketchup-Face, "there's an elephant in the room."

"Yes," said Stinkbomb, "but apparently you're not meant to talk about it. I'm not sure why."

"As you can see," continued Harry the Badger, "we've made the biggest water rocket in the world, and we've tied King Toothbrush Weasel to it.

It just needs one more pump to send it zooming out the window and far away."

He pointed at the big window at the back of the warehouse, in case anyone wasn't sure what windows looked like. "Then, in the next story, with all the good guys out of the way, we'll get to be the good guys."

"I still don't think it works like that," muttered Stewart the Badger unhappily.

"But the good guys aren't all out of the way, are they?" asked Samuel Neck.

"Yes they are!" said Harry the Badger. "We've defeated King Toothbrush Weasel by tying him to a giant water rocket; and we've defeated Stinkbomb and Ketchup-Face by tying them up and throwing them in the river; and we've defeated the librarians by messing up all the books in the library so it'll take them ages to put 'em all back in their proper places; and we've defeated the army by giving it a dish of cat food."

"Yum," agreed Malcolm the Cat from the front of the stage.

"So," Harry the Badger cried, "we win!"

CHAPTER 60

—•—

IN WHICH THE EXCITING CLIMAX OF THE STORY ACTUALLY HAPPENS

N o, you don't!" called Stinkbomb, as he, Ketchup-Face, and the rabbit pushed their way to the front.

"**Grrr!**" growled Harry the Badger. "Yes, we do!" he added, as several of the badgers leapt forward and grabbed them.

"No, you don't!" insisted Stinkbomb, as the badgers who had grabbed hold of the rabbit let go again, yelping with pain, and began sucking their paws. "We have gone on a quest to Stupidity and brought back this Magic Porcupine to put an end to your **evil** plans!"

"But . . . that's not a Magic Porcupine!" said King Toothbrush Weasel from above them. "It's a . . ."

"Yes, yes, all *right!*" said the rabbit in a fury, tearing off its **spiky** coat and flinging it down on the stage.

"Oh," said King Toothbrush Weasel. "It *is* a Magic Porcupine after all. I got confused because it was wearing a **spiky** coat that made it look like a dolphin."

"Well, whatever it is," growled Harry the Badger, "it doesn't have any real magic, so it can't do anything to stop us."

"Maybe I can't," admitted the rabbit, "but would you like to see some magic tricks anyway?"

"Oooh, yes, please!"

shouted the audience.

The badgers looked at each other and shrugged. "Might as well," said Rolf the Badger.

"Goody!" said Stewart the Badger.

"Right," said the rabbit. "For my first trick, I need some volunteers. **Evil** and **wicked** volunteers. Black-and-white ones, preferably."

"Us!" said the badgers excitedly.

"*Hmmm,*" said the rabbit. "Okay." And it pulled a pack of cards from behind Rolf the Badger's ear.

"Ooooh!"

went everybody.

"Now," the rabbit said to the badgers. "Pick a card. Any card. But don't look at it."

Each badger took a card and held it facedown. Stinkbomb and Ketchup-Face held their breath, hoping the Clever Plan would work.

"Now," said the rabbit, "look at your cards." The badgers did so. Their faces fell.

"Awwwww!" they said.

The rabbit looked suddenly very pleased with itself. "Show everyone your cards," it said.

"Do we *have* to?" whined the badgers.

"Yes," the rabbit said. "You volunteered."

"All *right*," sighed the badgers, and they held up the cards. As if by magic, each was now an identical peach-colored card on which was printed a little picture of a barred window and the words:

"Do we *have* to?" the badgers asked again.

"Yes, you do, you naughty badgers!" said Ketchup-Face triumphantly, and Stinkbomb added, "So there!"

"Come along," said a cheerful voice from the crowd. It was Mr. Jolly. "I'll take you there right now, you little scamps."

"Be careful they don't escape," said Stinkbomb. "It's just the sort of evil and wicked thing they *would* do."

"No chance of that, young master," Mr. Jolly assured him happily. "I'll take a couple of the other bus drivers along with me to keep an eye on them. I reckon Mr. Big and Mr. Scary ought to keep them in order. And maybe Mr. Useless."

Then he rubbed his chin. "Actually," he said confidentially, "maybe I won't take Mr. Useless. He's a bit . . . well . . ."

"Is anybody going to get me down from here?" King Toothbrush Weasel snapped.

"That cat food was nice," said Malcolm the Cat, licking his whiskers and stepping backward. "*Ouch,*" he added, standing on the **spiky** coat and leaping off again . . .

. . . only to land, to everyone's horror, on the pump. With a **bang!** and a tremendous

the gigantic water rocket shot
toward the window—

with King Toothbrush
Weasel still tied firmly to it.

CHAPTER 61

— • —

IN WHICH
ALL ENDS WELL

Eeeek!" squealed King Toothbrush Weasel, and then everything happened in a blur.

In the instant before the water rocket struck the great window of the warehouse, the glass shattered from the *outside*. A **tall** figure dressed in black somersaulted gracefully through it. In

a single elegant movement she drew
her sword, cut through the ropes that
held the king, and seized him in her arms.
Turning in the air, she dropped silently down
and landed, light as a feather, on the stage.

"OW," said Malcolm the Cat.

"Oh, sorry," said Miss Butterworth, looking
down and taking her foot off Malcolm the Cat's
tail.

"My hero!" said King Toothbrush Weasel, and

fainted. Then he unfainted for a moment, just to say, "Miss Butterworth, I mean; not Malcolm the Cat," and fainted again.

And so everything ended happily, and as night drew in, joyous and peaceful sounds could be heard all over the tiny kingdom of Great Kerfuffle.

In Stupidity, there was the sound of a slightly **sniffly** Magic Porcupine being tucked in and having a bedtime story.

In the Loose Pebbles Library, there was the sound of Miss Tibbles making all the badgers put the books back in their correct places before Mr. Jolly and his friends took them back to jail—the badgers, that is, not the books.

In a hedge by the road that runs along the River Yuk, there was the sound of animals watching TV together; a sudden **"Whoopee!";** a burst of joyful **scampering** through the undergrowth; a happy cry of, "I've won! I'm rich! I'm rich!"; a **crackle** of lightning; a **squeaky "OW!"** and then a **thump** and a complaint of "**Ouch!** My toe! Who left that asteroid there?"

And in Loose Pebbles, outside the old deserted warehouse next to the river, the famous Magic Rabbit of Stupidity was giving conjuring lessons to a hammerhead shark, a king, a well-fed army, a Ninja Librarian, a little shopping cart, and a very contented Stinkbomb and Ketchup-Face, who felt that only one more thing could make the evening absolutely perfect.

Then a boat came **chugging** up the river, and Felicity joyfully cried, "Captain Bonkers!"

"Ah-haar, me sharky!"

Captain Bonkers replied happily. "Would you believe, the whole island ran out of bananas, so I sailed off to get you some more! And on me way back upstream, I picked up a couple of passengers . . ."

Stinkbomb's and Ketchup-Face's hearts leapt as they saw two familiar shapes silhouetted in the cabin's window. And the door began to open.

"MOM! DAD!"

cried Stinkbomb.

"Hello, my darlings!" came their mother's voice from inside the cabin. "Can we come out? Has the story finished yet?"

"Yes!" said Ketchup-Face happily.

"WOULD YOU like to see a magic trick?"

How to Do a Magic Trick

by Ketchup-Face

 First you need a volunteer. Parents are good for this sort of thing even if they do tut and sigh and say "Oh all right but be quick 'cause I have to send this email by five o'clock."

 Get the volunteer to pick a card, show it to you, and put it back in the pack.

 Point behind them and say, "Gosh! Look at that!" in a gosh-look-at-that kind of voice.

 Get your brother to do something really interesting just where you're pointing, like dancing in a funny way or juggling fruit or teaching a lion to ride a bicycle. If you haven't got a brother, a king or a librarian will do.

While the volunteer is looking at the interesting something, look through the pack until you find their card.

 Stick the card behind their ear without them noticing. If they've got sticky-out ears, you might have to use tape or glue or chewing gum. (If you use chewing gum, try not to get it stuck in their hair 'cause if they find out you'll get in trouble. If they don't find out, then the next morning they'll probably have a pillow stuck to their head.)

 Tell your brother to stop doing the interesting thing, even if he's at the best part.

 Pull the card from behind the volunteer's ear.

 Ta-paaaa!
It's their card. Magic!

ACKNOWLEDGMENTS

Once more, thanks to all those children from whose games and foolery I've magpied bits of this book.

And "hello" to everyone at West Earlham Junior School, where I used to be Patron of Reading, and to all at Minchinhampton Primary, where I'm Patron of Reading now. Don't know what a Patron of Reading is? Find out at www.patronofreading.co.uk.

KEEP READING FOR A GLIMPSE OF THE NEXT KERFUFFLE!

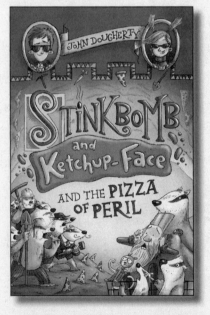

CHAPTER 1

——·——

IN WHICH
OUR HEROES WAKE UP,
AND SOME STUFF HAPPENS

It was the quietest hour, when night covers the world like a blanket. Above the peaceful little island of Great Kerfuffle, stars **shimmered** like silver sequins against the velvet blackness. Below, the earth was silent. Not a creature stirred; all was still.

Then the sun popped **up** over the horizon like a jolly potato, and morning started.

And in a tall tree in the yard of a lovely house high on a hillside above the tiny village of Loose

Pebbles, a blackbird, was **singing** in the shower. Trees don't usually have showers, of course, but the blackbird wanted to be clean for the start of the story, so it had had one installed.

Inside the lovely house, in a beautiful pink bedroom, a little girl called Ketchup-Face was sleeping peacefully . . . until the blackbird turned the tap all the way up to "extra splooshy" and began **twittering** at the top of its voice. At that, Ketchup-Face stopped sleeping peacefully and jumped out of bed, extremely unpeacefully.

"Hey!
BLACKBIRD!

Zip it!"

she yelled, running toward the window. **"Ow,"** she added, as the soap the blackbird had just thrown at her bounced off her forehead.

"Waaaaaauuugggghh!" she continued as she stepped on the soap and, arms waving frantically, skidded across the room. **"Oof,"** she concluded, banging her nose against the window frame.

The blackbird, grinning hugely, stuck out its tongue and blew a **raspberry**. Then it rinsed off the suds, turned off the shower, dried itself with a little towel, and flew away.

Rubbing her nose, Ketchup-Face went to wake her brother.

Ketchup-Face's brother was named Stinkbomb, and seconds later he woke to find his sister trying to tie a knot in his legs.

"What," he demanded grumpily, "are you doing?"

"I'm trying to tie a knot in your legs," Ketchup-Face explained.

"Why?" Stinkbomb grouched.

"To see if I can," Ketchup-Face answered, frowning and poking her tongue out of the corner of her mouth.

Stinkbomb thought about this. The idea of having a knot tied in his legs certainly sounded interesting, but he wasn't sure if he would actually like it. So he decided to throw a pillow at his sister.

"Oof," said Ketchup-Face through a faceful of pillow, falling over backward. "What did you do that for?"

"I don't want you to tie a knot in my legs," Stinkbomb explained.

"Why not?"

"Because if there's a knot in my legs, I won't be able to put my pants on. And if we have an adventure when there's a knot in my legs, I won't be able to run away from the bad guys."

"Okay," said Ketchup-Face, getting up. "Do you think we're going to have an adventure?"

"I should think so," said Stinkbomb wisely. "It feels like that sort of story."

And just then, there was a **knock** on the door.

CHAPTER 2

— • —

IN WHICH
THE DOOR IS ANSWERED,
AND THE ADVENTURE BEGINS

Only thirteen words later, Stinkbomb and Ketchup-Face had shoved themselves into their clothes. Racing to the front door, they flung it open. There, on the threshold, was a little shopping cart wearing a pair of dark glasses.

"Starlight!" Ketchup-Face said delightedly. "My horsey!"

"*Shhh!*" **hissed** the little shopping cart. "I don't want anyone to know it's me! I'm in disguise!"

Stinkbomb looked around carefully, and

then leaned closer. "But your name isn't really Starlight," he pointed out quietly. "And you're not really a horsey."

"You could pretend to be," added Ketchup-Face in a cheerful whisper. "If you don't want people to know it's you."

"Fair point," the little shopping cart admitted after a moment's thought. Then, more loudly, it added, "Er, yes, that's right. It's me, Starlight. The, er, horsey. **Whinny, whinny, neigh, neigh.** Um . . . got any carrots?"

"I might," Stinkbomb said, feeling around in his pockets. Stinkbomb was the sort of boy who kept all kinds of useful things in his pockets, and quite a lot of useless things as well. "Yes, here you are." He produced a large carrot and jammed it between two of the wires of the basket, a little below the sunglasses.

"Thanks," said the little shopping cart. "Er . . . yum. I love carrots. **Neigh, whinny, whinny, neigh.** I'm a horse. All right, hop in."

Stinkbomb and Ketchup-Face scrambled into

the basket, and seconds later they were galloping across the fields like two children in a little shopping cart.

"Why the disguise?" Stinkbomb wanted to know.

"Well," the little shopping cart said modestly, "I'm doing a job for the Great Kerfuffle **Secret Service**."

"**Wow!**" said Stinkbomb, impressed. Then, feeling that this didn't convey just *how* impressed he was, he said, "**Wowsers!**" This still didn't seem quite enough, so after a moment's thought he added, **"WOWsers my trousers!"**

This felt more like it. "So, where are we going?"

"We're going to the headquarters of the Great Kerfuffle **Secret Service**," the little shopping cart whispered, and just at that moment they drew up outside King Toothbrush Weasel's palace. Pinned to the gate was a piece of paper on which someone had written:

Headquarters
of the
Great Kerfuffle
Secret Service

King Toothbrush Weasel was the king of the little island of Great Kerfuffle, and his palace was about the size of a small cottage. It had pretty little towers with thatched turrets, and dinky little battlements, and the sweetest little sentry box you've ever seen. The sentry box was usually full of the entire army of Great Kerfuffle, who was a small cat named Malcolm the Cat, but at the moment it was empty. As the little shopping cart **screeched** to a halt in what it hoped was a daring and **secret-agentish** sort of way, Stinkbomb and Ketchup-Face leapt from its basket and ran to the door.

"Wait!" the little shopping cart said. "They won't let you in unless you do the **secret knock**!"

"Wowsers my trousers!" said Stinkbomb, feeling that this adventure was getting more exciting by the minute, and hoping that before long it would involve **disguises** and **gadgets** and **foreign spies**. "What's the **secret knock**?"

The little shopping cart shrugged. "I don't know," it said. "It's a **secret**."

Ketchup-Face waved her fist very near to the door without touching it. "That's a **secret knock**," she said. "It's so **secret** you can't even hear it."

"But if nobody can hear it," said Stinkbomb, "how will the person on the other side of the door know you've **knocked**?"

Ketchup-Face scratched her head. "Um . . . don't know," she said cheerily. "Why don't you try?"

"Okay," agreed Stinkbomb. Thinking hard, he raised his hand to the knocker and **knocked** the most **secret** and complicated **knock** he could think of. It went:

Knock . . .

Knock-knock knockity knock . . .

Knock kno-knock knock-knock-knock . . .

Knock-knock, knock-knock, knock knock knockity knock knock knock . . .

Knock knock kno-knock knock, knock kno-knock kno-knock . . .

Knock knock knock knock . . . knock . . .
Knock knock knock,
knockkkkkk knockkkkkk knockkkk,
knock knock knock . . .

. . .

Knock knock . . .

. . .

. . . knock . . .

Knock!!!!!!
Knock!!!!!!!
knock!!!!!!

. . . knock knock knock knock knock knock
knock knock knock knock . . .

Tap tap tippity tippity tap tap tap . . .

Knock knock

Tap

Knock knock

Tap

Knock knock

Tap tap tippity tippity tap tap tap

Knock knock kno-knock knock knock,
knocky knock knock, knock knock . . .

. . .

. . .

. . .

. . .

. . .

. . .

. . .

. . .

. . .

. . .

...

...

...

...

...

...

...

...

...

...

...

...

...

Knock.

He stood back, like an artist admiring his work, and then, after a moment's thought, stepped back up to the door, lifted the knocker again, and added:

Knock kno-kno-knock knock, knock knock!

Then he stood back again, folded his arms, and waited.

CHAPTER 3

——— • ———

IN WHICH
THE DOOR IS ANSWERED

Very soon there came a voice from behind
the door.

"Was that the **secret knock**?" it said.

"Yes," said Stinkbomb.

"Oh," said the voice. "I didn't think the **secret
knock** was as long as that."

"Well, it is," Stinkbomb said. "I did it brilliantly,
didn't I?"

"Yes," said the voice. "I don't know how you
managed to remember it all."

"Actually," said Stinkbomb, "I might have gone a bit wrong in the middle. Shall I do it again?"

"Er, no, that's all right," the voice said quickly.

The door opened and there, wearing a pair of dark glasses, a serious expression, and a little badge, stood King Toothbrush Weasel.

"Hello, King Toothbrush Weasel," said Ketchup-Face brightly.

King Toothbrush Weasel gave her a stern look. "I am not King Toothbrush Weasel," he said firmly. He pointed at his badge, which said Head of Palace Security , and said, "I am the Head of Palace Security." Then he looked at the little shopping cart. "Why have you got a carrot jammed into the front of your basket?"

"It's a disguise," the shopping cart said.

King Toothbrush Weasel's forehead wrinkled in puzzlement. "Why have you disguised yourself as a carrot?"

"Er, no," the little shopping cart said shyly, "I'm disguised as a horse. **Neigh, whinny, neigh.**"

"A *horse*?"
said King
Toothbrush Weasel.
"Horses don't have carrots jammed in the front of
their baskets."

"I'm pretending to eat it," explained the shopping cart.

King Toothbrush Weasel shook his head impatiently. "Horses don't eat carrots," he said. "They
eat goldfish."

"No they don't!" protested Ketchup-Face.

"Yes they do," insisted King Toothbrush Weasel.
"The horse climbs **up** a tree and sits on a branch,
waiting for a nice fat goldfish to come **trotting**
along, and when it does, the horse drops **down**
out of the tree onto the goldfish and eats it up."

"I think you're thinking of jaguars," said

Stinkbomb politely. "But they drop onto deer, not goldfish."

"No," said King Toothbrush Weasel. "Jaguars don't *eat* deer; they turn *into* them. The deer lays eggs in a sort of jelly, which is called deerspawn, and they hatch out into jaguars, which swim around the pond until they grow legs and their tails drop off and they turn into deer."

"No, you silly king," Ketchup-Face said. "That's not jaguars and deers, it's frogs and **Ow!** what did

you do that for? I only said it was **ow!"**
she added as Stinkbomb elbowed her in the ribs
again.

"Let's not stand here arguing about animals,"
Stinkbomb hissed. "I want to get on with the
adventure."

"Okay," Ketchup-Face said. "I only said it was

 okay, okay, let's get on
with the adventure."

"Very well," agreed King Toothbrush Weasel.
"You'd better come in."